SPOOKTON VILLAGE

A RHYMING PICTURE BOOK

Thank you for supporting an independent author. If you purchased this book through a platform that allows reviews, please would you consider doing so to assist the author.

CFAL

Published by CFAL Print

ISBN 978-1-0672599-3-8

cfalprint@gmail.com
Facebook Page: Tarryn C Roberts - Author
https://tarryncandice.wixsite.com/tarryn-c-roberts---a

For families who love
all things spooky

Gather round, children
There's a creep in the air
This story is spooky
And told with such flair

In a village called Spookton

Where the ghosts roam

The weird and the wonderful
Call this their home

Some houses are pleasant
And not so creepy
Their owners are friendly
But no one gets sleepy

Some houses are eerie
They are dark and scary
The creatures that live there
Can be a bit hairy

But the big scary house

Has something so great

It has hundreds of books

We can read till it's late

Let's go through this arch
To see where it leads
It could bring us trouble
Or lead to bad deeds

We're now in the graveyard

Watch where you tread

The ones who sleep here

Are not fully dead

There's skeleton families
And their little kitties

They prefer the quiet
And not the big cities

There are ghosts at night
Who wander around

They like to say "BOO!"

It is their best sound

Even the mummies
Who also live there

Will try their best
To give you a scare

Thank you for visiting
Now be on your way

These are the other books by the author which are the
Emily's Adventures book series

EMILY'S ADVENTURES:
WHERE'S MY DOLLY?
BY
TARRYN C ROBERTS

EMILY'S ADVENTURES:
EXPLORING THE GARDEN
BY
TARRYN C ROBERTS

EMILY'S ADVENTURES:
ANIMAL ALPHABET
BY
TARRYN C ROBERTS

EMILY'S ADVENTURES:
LET'S PLAY DRESS-UP
BY
TARRYN C ROBERTS

Other children's books by the author

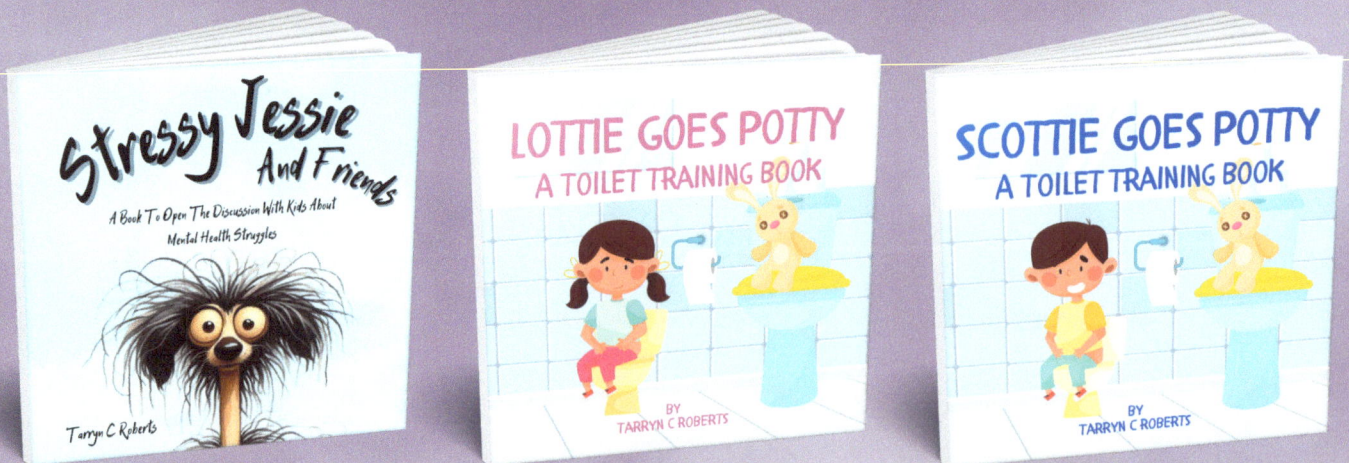

Stressy Jessie
And Friends
A Book To Open The Discussion With Kids About
Mental Health Struggles
Tarryn C Roberts

LOTTIE GOES POTTY
A TOILET TRAINING BOOK
BY
TARRYN C ROBERTS

SCOTTIE GOES POTTY
A TOILET TRAINING BOOK
BY
TARRYN C ROBERTS

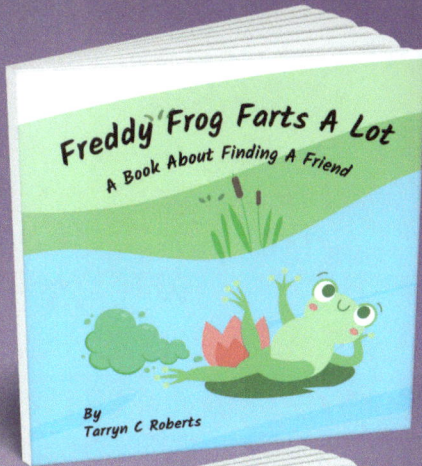

Freddy Frog Farts A Lot

A Book About Finding A Friend

By
Tarryn C Roberts

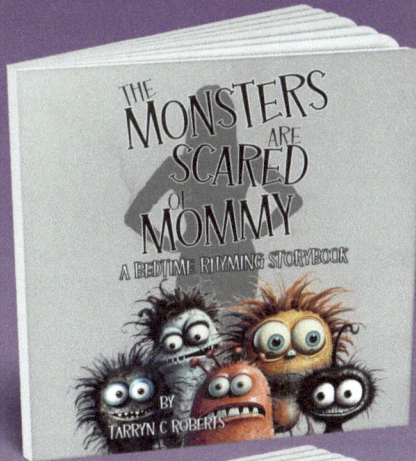

THE MONSTERS ARE SCARED of MOMMY

A BEDTIME RHYMING STORYBOOK

BY
TARRYN C ROBERTS

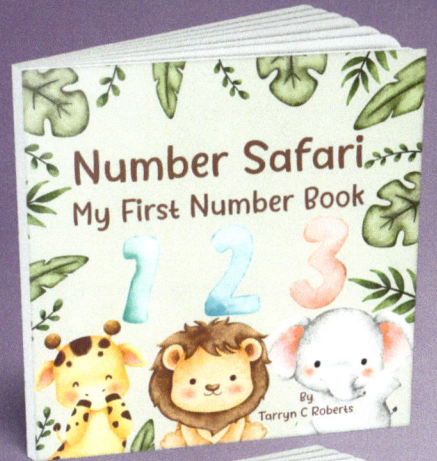

Number Safari

My First Number Book

1 2 3

BY
Tarryn C Roberts

This Little Monster Felt Happy

Identifying Emotions For Little Ones

BY
Tarryn C Roberts

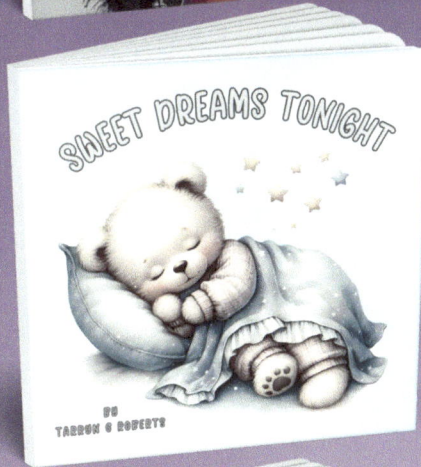

SWEET DREAMS TONIGHT

BY
TARRYN C ROBERTS

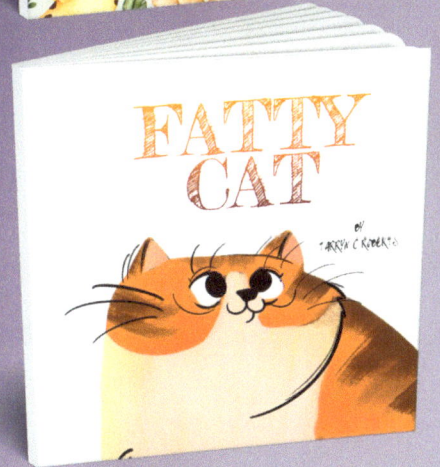

FATTY CAT

BY
TARRYN C ROBERTS

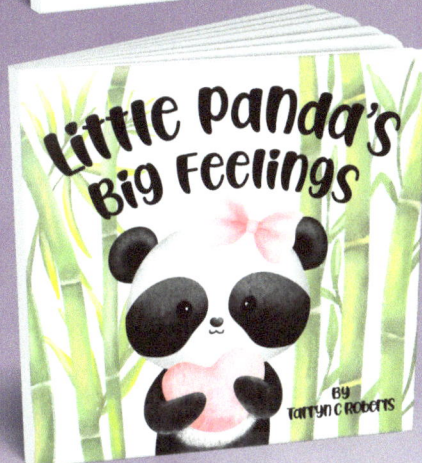

Little Panda's Big Feelings

BY
Tarryn C Roberts

www.ingramcontent.com/pod-product-compliance
Lightning Source LLC
LaVergne TN
LVHW072100070426
835508LV00002B/198